Spy dogs 0

The Beginning

Amma Lee

INTRODUCTION

"The Beginning" strays away from the main character, Puggy from the spy dogs series, by bringing in a cute little Pomeranian named Harper. Harper is one of the dogs that were kidnapped by the aliens, Zork and Cyze, in the first three stories. This prequel tells the tale of little Harper and his owners, Joseph and Jessica. Harper thought he would have a fun vacation with Joseph, but he was proven wrong when Jessica tried to call all of the shots, leading Harper to escape their cabin which ultimately gets him captured. This side story featuring Harper tells the story of how everything came to be and how spy dogs was created.

CHAPTER ONE

"Stop whining, we're almost there." Jessica said as she carried Joseph's precious Pomeranian, Harper, in her arms.

"He's probably hungry," Joseph said as he walked in front of the two. Joseph had decided to take Jessica and Harper camping since the weather was so good. Harper was incredibly irritable. To be just a small dog, he thrashed around wildly in Jessica's arms.

"How much further do we have before we're there?" Joseph stopped in his tracks and looked around, scratching his beard.

"I don't know. Maybe a half of a mile," Jessica sighed, but she continued walking. It had been awhile since they had been on vacation. The last time they went on vacation had been shortly before Joseph and Jessica got married and that was almost three years ago. Harper really wanted to be put down. He wanted to feel the mud on his paws and smell the scent of the new land. Harper was irritable because he wished that they were at the location already. He was also irritable because Jessica was clinging onto him.

"I know what you want," Jessica said and reached a hand into her pants pocket and pulled out some small glasses. "Here you go," she said as she placed the glasses on Harper's face. He whined, he didn't like the object that she placed on his face. It made him feel weird. He reached up his paw to try to push it off of his face. "No, no, no," Jessica cooed and grabbed his paw lightly. "You need to wear those; your eyes aren't the best. Don't you want to see better?"

"You're making him mad Jess, why don't you put him down for a little while?" Joseph said as he turned back to look at Harper. Jessica shook her head.

"He loves being in my arms." Harper couldn't have disagreed more. Harper didn't mind being held by his owners, but when they held him when he wanted to run around, that's when it became a problem.

"Jess," Joseph said again and Jessica sighed, but she put the cute little Pomeranian down on the ground. The second Harper's paws touched the ground; he stood on his hind legs and began bouncing around. He was finally free to explore the earth with his nose. "I told you he wanted to be put down. Look at how happy he is now." Jessica folded her arms.

"I guess you were right," she muttered under her breath

and Joseph grinned. The three of them walked on for another thirty minutes before they saw Joseph's uncle's cabin in the middle of the woods. Recognizing the place immediately, Harper ran over to the house and barked for his owners to hurry up.

"Geez, hold on Harper, we're coming." Joseph said as he ran over to his dog. Joseph could see how excited Harper was and it made him excited too. When Joseph was near Harper, he knelt down in front of him. "Give me paw!" Joseph said cheerfully and Harper barked and placed his paw into Joseph's hand.
"The mutt likes you just fine," Jessica said, placing her hands on her hips.

"It's because I've had him since he was a baby. It normally takes Harper a few years to get used to someone. He'll get used to you soon." Joseph said as he unlocked the door to the cabin. It was hot inside and full of cobwebs, but other than that it looked the same. It had gotten darker since they'd been walking and even though there was still some light outside, it was close to pitch black in the house.

"Where's the light switch at?"

"It should be on the wall." Jessica rubbed her hands on the wall until she found the light switch. She turned it upward and was happy to be presented with light. Harper ran around the small cabin, it was the same way that he remembered and his scratch marks still covered the wall where his dog bowl was normally at.

3

"This is a nice place; it needs to be cleaned up though." Jessica said as she walked further into the cabin. She tried to pick Harper up again, but he quickly dodged her when she reached down to grab him.

"Of course it needs cleaning," Joseph said in a matter-a-fact way. "No one's been here in three years." Harper wasn't paying any attention to either one of them. Harper ran into the bathroom and looked into the toilet and then ran into the bedroom and went under the bed. He played with some lent that made its home under the bed before he went back into the living room and barked.

"I'll get him some food." Jessica said as she walked into the kitchen that was adjourned with the living room. She looked into the cabinet and pulled out a rather beat up looking bowl. She grabbed one of the bags that Joseph had sat on the floor and looked for some food. She poured some into the bowl and sat it down. Harper ran straight towards it and pushed it into his favorite corner. "What is he doing?" Jessica asked surprised, as she watched Harper push the bowl towards the wall.

"He likes eating over there for some reason. I wouldn't have actually expected him to still do that though." After the bowl was as close to the wall as possible, Harper began woofing down his food.

"He acts like he hasn't eaten in years," Jessica said, eyeing the dog in wonder.

"Maybe a few hours are years to a dog," Joseph suggested and shrugged his shoulders. "Let me show you around since this is your first time here." Joseph showed Jessica around the place and left Harper alone to fend for himself. Harper ran into the living room and jumped on the couch. He looked out of the window remembering the last time Joseph and he had been there.

He was still a young pup and he remembered their trip as being magical. He was kind of sad that Joseph had invited Jessica along with them this year. This trip was supposed to be just for Joseph and him, but Harper understood that she'd be in the picture for a long time now, so he needed to accept this fact.

As Harper was looking out of the window at the sky, he saw a strange object flying in the air. This was unlike any object that he'd ever seen before. It was quite a distance away, but he knew for a fact that the object was big. He saw a light coming from it and he noticed the light shone brightly in the house. He jumped off of the couch and covered his eyes.

The brightness of the light irritated his eyes. When he jumped back into the window, the object in the sky was gone! He didn't know what to think about it, so Harper settled for it being a crazy invention that the humans had come up with.

He heard his owners talking in the other room and he decided that it was time for him to go to sleep. It was going to be a long day for him tomorrow and he had a lot of things planned. First he was going to eat his food, then he'd run outside for a little while. After he was done running, he'd go for a swim and it'll be good if Joseph joined him. Harper walked around in a circle on the floor next to the couch and then balled himself up. Barking silently, Harper hoped that tomorrow would be full of fun.

CHAPTER TWO

Harper woke up bright and early the next morning and he was happy to see some light out of the window. He jumped up and shook his matted fur and ran into Joseph's room. The two humans were still sleeping so Harper took it upon himself to wake them up. Harper jumped onto the bed and began barking.

"Get the dog," Jessica mumbled as she pulled the sheet over her face. Joseph didn't stir though. Harper continued barking and jumping on Joseph. "Joseph!" Jessica shouted this time, sounding quite angry.

"Huh?" Joseph said quite sleepily.

"Get the dog," Joseph was so used to Harper barking at any time of the day, that he honestly didn't realize that he was barking. Joseph sighed and got out from under the covers and grabbed the Pomeranian.

"Hey buddy," he said yawning and walking Harper out of the bedroom. He grabbed the dog food and poured it into Harper's bowl. Picking up the water bowl next to Harper's food bowl, Joseph refilled it with some cool and fresh water. Joseph yawned again and made his way back to the bedroom.

"Try to keep it down; it's not just us anymore." Joseph said just before he closed the bedroom door. Harper whined. He really wanted to play with Joseph before Jessica woke up. Barking one last time, he moved his mouth to devour his food.

Once his bowl was empty and his belly was full, Harper walked over to the corner of the cabin. There was a loose board somewhere in the corner that he used to get out of the house. Searching for it for a few minutes, his nose finally hit the piece of board that he was looking for.

Barking happily, he took the board into his small mouth and threw the wood aside. Finally! He was outside! The air was cool and dew was misted onto the grass, Harper absolutely loved coming outside first thing in the morning.

The birds was chirping and picking up twigs off of the ground. Harper ran over to them and they flew away quickly. Harper was having a lot of fun. He wanted to go swimming now, but he wanted to go swimming with Joseph so he told himself to wait till Joseph was ready.

Joseph didn't allow Harper to swim by himself because the last time he did, Harper got stuck on something and was stuck for almost an hour before Joseph realized it. Harper was tired of trying to set himself free, but he didn't feel like he was in any type of danger.

Harper ran over to the water and stuck his paw into it. It was cold and a magical blue color. Harper looked at his reflection in the water and barked when he noticed that he was still wearing the object that the humans called "glasses." He didn't mind them being on him, but sometimes it did irritate his nose.

He also didn't mind them too much because it did help him see a little better. As he was admiring his reflection, a frog on a lily pad floated by him. Harper looked at the frog and the frog looked at Harper. Harper barked and the frog jumped into the water.

Forgetting about waiting for Joseph to join him, Harper jumped into the water after the frog. He had just found a new plaything and he didn't want to lose it that quickly. The frog was faster than him in the water and eventually gotten away. Feeling defeated, Harper swam back to the shore.

The brisk air was starting to get to Harper now and its chilly wind kissed his wet fur. Shivering, Harper ran back into the house and placed the board back into its original spot. As soon it was back in place, Jessica walked out into the living room and gasped.

"How did you get so wet?" she asked as she headed straight towards Harper. Harper was unsuccessful this time when she tried to grab him. She held Harper fast and took him into the bathroom.

"Did you get into the toilet?" Jessica said as she noted that the toilet lid was open. Thinking that was the only way that Harper could have gotten soaked, she placed the toilet seat and lid down. "Bad dog" she said as she grabbed a towel and began drying off Harper's fur.

Joseph came out of the bedroom then and looked over at Jessica and Harper. "What happened here?" Joseph asked looking at the irritated Pomeranian.

"I think he got into the toilet somehow. When I saw him he was soaked from head to toe." Jessica said still patting down Harper's fur. He really just wanted to get away from her to greet Joseph. Joseph was probably ready to play with him now and Harper wanted to take this opportunity before Joseph decided to do something else with his time.

"You don't have to do that. He'll shake his fur until he's dry." Jessica scowled at him.

"You let this dog walk all over you. It's time to set some ground rules for him." Joseph sighed and walked out of the bathroom to start working on breakfast. As soon as Jessica took the towel from him and loosened her grip, Harper leapt out of her arms and made his way into the kitchen. He ran over to Joseph's feet and barked. Joseph looked down at Harper and smiled.

"Sorry boy, but you can't have any of this food. I have to put my foot down. You heard Jessica," Harper shook his fur. He couldn't have cared less about the human food that Joseph was preparing. Harper wanted to go outside. He wanted to go swimming and running with Joseph. Harper bit at his pants leg trying to pull Joseph in the direction of the door.

"I just bought you those pajamas, Joe!" Jessica said coming out of the bathroom. Joseph picked up Harper and walked him into the living room and placed him on the couch. He mouthed 'sorry buddy' and went back into the kitchen. Harper was furious! He couldn't have Joseph for himself for five minutes before Jessica came out and ruined their fun. Harper began jumping on the couch and whined loudly.

"Harper…" Joseph said in a warning voice. This just made Harper bark louder.

"You see!" Jessica said walking over to Harper. "You've spoiled him and now he thinks he can do whatever he wants." She reached down to grab Harper, but he jumped out of Jessica's reach and growled at her.

"Harper," Joseph said louder. He didn't know what had gotten into Harper but he could tell that he was getting incredibly irritated with Jessica. Joseph turned off the stove and walked over to Harper and grabbed him before he could run away.

"What is wrong with you? You don't growl at Jessica," Joseph placed Harper down on the bed in the bedroom and turned around and walked through the door. "You're on time out until further notice." Harper began barking even louder. He didn't want to be stuck in this room; he wanted to be outside with Joseph.

Harper ran around the room wondering what he needed to do to get out of the room. He ran and scratched at the door, leaving his small scratches at the bottom of the door. When that didn't work, Harper barked louder. He could hear Joseph and Jessica talking in the front, but he couldn't make out what they were saying. Harper began whining again.

Joseph had betrayed him. He had thrown away their friendship because of that other human. He no longer felt appreciated by Joseph and he was starting to think that he'd be in that room forever. Harper looked around the room and noticed a cool breeze coming from the window.

He jumped on top of the chair that was directly in front of the window and then he jumped on the desk. The window was opened and thankfully there wasn't anything keeping him inside. The gap was a little small so Harper had to squeeze himself through the window.

Harper jumped from the window sill and landed without incident onto the ground. He looked behind him at the house, if Joseph wanted to treat Harper unkindly; he'd treat him unkindly too. With that said, Harper disappeared into the woods.

CHAPTER THREE

Harper ran as fast as he could until he was sure that he was out of sight. He wouldn't let them win and have him locked away in some room when he wanted to play. He'd swim by himself and run around by himself. He'd have so much fun by himself that he wouldn't care that he'd be in trouble when he got back to them.

He'd swim around in the water and eat berries. Joseph never let him eat any berries. He'd play in the mud and chase after the birds. Harper was running so fast that he almost lost his footing and fell. When he finally stopped, he couldn't even see the cabin anymore.

Deciding to slow down and look at the scenery, Harper happily played with the bumble bees that were flying around a sunflower. There were a lot of colorful flowers and Harper had a great time pouncing on them. Harper saw fish jumping out of the water and he thought that it would be a great idea to jump in the water as well.

The water was just as cold as it was a few hours ago.

The fish jumped so high out of the water that Harper thought they were trying to challenge him. He leapt up as high as he could and came back into the water with a loud splash!

Harper loved the water and he wished that Joseph was there, but Joseph wanted to spend all of his time with the human and not with him. Swimming back to the shore, Harper shook his fur and sat down and stared into the mass of water. He felt peaceful and at ease. The sun was getting brighter and he started to think that they'd come looking for him soon. He wouldn't let them get him just yet though; he wouldn't let them take all of his fun away.

Harper got up and began walking even further into the woods. He'd never walked this far by himself, but he was sure that he'd be able to find his way back home when he was ready to go back. He thought he heard someone calling his name from far away, but he shook his head, there was no way that Joseph and Jessica would have caught up that quickly.

Harper walked a little further until the green ground became rocky. Was he no longer in the forest? Harper jumped down from a large rock that he didn't even know that he was on and stopped short when he saw several other dogs walking down the path. He barked with glee! He'd be able to play with these dogs since Joseph didn't want to play with him.

Harper began running again in the direction of the dogs

when he saw an odd creature come out of nowhere.

"I've let you walk long enough!" he heard the creature say. It was odd, Harper thought that the thing sounded like a human, but it looked so much different than one. It was pink and gooey looking. He didn't like it! The dogs went towards the creature in an almost dazed state. With one look at the way the animals were acting, he knew that something was seriously wrong. He crouched down in some shrubbery and watched the pink creature in awe.

"What have we here?" Harper jumped when he heard a voice from behind him. He turned around quickly and barked when he saw a similar creature behind him. The only difference was this one was blue!

"Cyze, this dog doesn't look like one of the one's that we took." The creature, Cyze, looked over into their direction and Harper jumped away when the new creature tried to grab him.

"Oh, he is definitely a new one. He must be lost out here. Should we take him, Zork?"

"The more the merrier," the creature called Zork said and bent down to try to grab Harper again. Harper jumped away from the creature again. Something was wrong here. These things were too eager to just take him.

Harper didn't know why, but he felt the strong urge to run and so he did. "Get back here!" the creature said when Harper turned around and began running away. This was bad, Harper made a bad decision when he left the house.

The land turned back green under his paws and he was starting to feel hopeful. If he could get back to the cabin, Joseph wouldn't let these things take him. When Harper turned around and looked over his shoulder, he was surprised to see the creature fast on his heels. "Ha! You're just a little shrimp, there's no way that you can outrun me for much longer."

He couldn't believe that this thing was able to keep up with him. He knew that he was a small dog, but neither Joseph nor Jessica was able to keep up with him when he was running. Harper ducked and dodged fallen trees and giant boulders, but even those obstacles didn't stop the creature that was chasing him.

Harper was starting to feel afraid. He didn't know what this thing was that was chasing him and he definitely did not want to find out. He was sorry that he made a lot of noise at the house and made Joseph and Jessica mad at him. He was sorry that he had left the house without their permission. He just wanted them to save him. Please save him!

"Got you!" the creature said and leapt onto Harper. Harper yelped and whined when the creature's body held his body down on the ground. The creature felt slimy and it smelled unlike anything Harper had ever smelled before. Harper struggled, wiggling under the weight of the creature, but it was pointless. The thing had him and it had him good.

"You're a little fighter," the creature said standing up with Harper gripped tightly in its clutches. "You'll definitely be a good dog to use for war, even if you're small." Did the creature just say war? Harper didn't know what 'war' meant, but he knew for certain that it was something bad and something that he didn't want anything to do with.

Harper barked and tried to bite the creature so that it would let go of him. The creature laughed and squeezed Harper's fur hard. Harper whined and stopped moving. This thing didn't care if he hurt Harper or not, so it would be best if he stopped fighting him.

"Harper!" he heard Joseph's voice and his ears popped up. They had come looking for him! They were going to save him. Just when Harper was about to bark, the creature held his mouth closed tightly with its hand.

"So Harper's your name?" the creature asked with a low tone. "Make a sound and I'll squeeze you again." Harper shivered, he did not want to be squeezed but he wanted to let Joseph know where he was at. When he decided that he'd face the consequences of being squeezed again, the creature pulled out something and pressed it.

Whatever it was, it made them start disappearing. This frightened Harper because he never knew that something like this could even happen. Just before they completely vanished, Harper saw Joseph and Jessica walk from behind some tall trees. Harper barked.

"Harper, where are you?" Joseph called out when he heard his dog's barks, but it was too late. The creature and Harper had already disappeared.

CHAPTER FOUR

"We have to move fast," Zork said appearing from the sky and landing hard on his feet with Harper still in his grip. "There's humans looking for this dog, they'll be here any minute now." Cyze's eyes widened and he pulled out a device and pushed a button. A rather large object took up majority of the ground a few feet in front of them. Harper barked. This was the same thing that Harper had seen in the sky the other night! Were these things inside of it with these dogs last night?

"Alright, give me the dog and I'll lead them inside." Harper began whining. He didn't want to go with these creatures! He just wanted to go home. Zork handed Harper to Cyze and Harper began barking. They weren't far away from where they had seen Joseph and Jessica. Harper needed them to hear him barking.

"Quiet the mutt before the humans hear him," Cyze got out a whistle and placed it up to its lips and blew. The sound of the whistle made the dogs howl in pain.

"If you don't want to hear this sound again, be quiet and do as I say." The other dogs whimpered, but made no other noises. Harper rubbed his ears with his paw and Cyze looked at him. "If you make any noise or continue to struggle, I'll make you regret it."

Harper shivered in fear. He did not want them to blow that whistle again nor did he want them to squeeze him. Cyze looked at Harper for a few more moments before he sat him down on the ground.

"March," Zork called out and walked in the direction of the large object. Harper didn't know what march meant, but he followed the other animal's movements. Harper kept his eyes low to the ground and he was feeling incredibly sad. There was no sign of Joseph nor Jessica anywhere around them and there was a strong possibility that they wouldn't get to Harper in time.

Harper looked up when the object began making noises. The noise was similar to the thing that humans called cars, so Harper started to suspect that the object was some type of vehicle. He was pushed into it quickly and felt unnerved because of how cold it was. It was pitch black and the only thing that he could see was the other dog's eyes.

"Is that all of them?" Zork asked pushing a button to close the entrance. Cyze began mumbling something under his breath.

"Yes, we have all of the animals plus one." Cyze laughed at this last remark and it made Harper furious, but there wasn't anything that he could do about it. He was pushed roughly from behind again so he reluctantly began moving his feet. The other dogs followed instructions without further prompting from the creatures. These things definitely had done something to them.

Harper heard noises that signaled that something was opening, but he couldn't quite make out the objects that were surrounding the animals. One by one, the animals went into them and they slammed down shut. It looked like a bigger version of what he was put into when he went on planes with Joseph. He thought they were called cages and if it was a cage, he knew that he did not like them.

"What are you waiting for?" Zork asked. "Get into the cage," Harper hesitated. He didn't want to get into it because he wouldn't be able to run around. He needed to be free to roam all over the place and not be stuck in one place. When Harper didn't go into the cage, he was shoved into one quickly and the door slammed shut in front of his face. Harper started barking frantically. "Do we have any more of that spray that would subdue this creature? It's becoming quite the nuisance."

Cyze pushed a few buttons on the dashboard located on a panel in front of him to make the spaceship go invisible. He thought for a few more moments. "There might be a little more left on the table behind you." Zork turned around and indeed found a spray bottle containing a substance that was powerful enough to make the animals obey them for a few hours.

"We need to hurry and find a place to make our base so that we can return this ship back to our brothers." Harper watched as Zork came back towards him shaking the bottle in its hand. Whatever was in the spray bottle, Harper did not want to be sprayed with it.

Harper moved his body as far back as possible to the back of the cage, but it was no use. The creature shook the bottle one more time and sprayed him. After a few moments, Harper lost a sense of his self and couldn't even remember the faces of Joseph and Jessica.

###

Harper couldn't remember when they landed and when they went inside of the house. His legs felt like Jell-O and his brain was fuzzy. He could feel his cage being carried into a room and placed down with a hard thump! He saw lights from weird screens being turned on which made him blink several times. His memory was coming back to him and unfortunately, so was his fear! He remembered being taken by those weird creatures after he had left the cabin without his owner's permission.

"It looks like the small dog over there is regaining control over his body," Harper looked through his cage's bars and saw the pink and blue creatures looking at him.

Harper began barking loudly."

"Ugh," Zork said rubbing its head. "This dog is a pain, maybe we should have left it behind."

"Brother, I believe this dog would be the perfect dog soldier. This dog is the only dog that put up such a huge resistance. This dog is stubborn, but we'll control him eventually." The two creatures smiled at each other, which made Harper bark louder. He wouldn't be controlled by anyone, but Joseph! Joseph \was the only one that was allowed to tell him what to do.

"Yes, but we need to do something about the barking. He might wake the humans on either side of us." Were they close to other humans? Was there a possibility that these people would hear Harper's barking and come over there? Harper didn't know the answers to this, so he barked louder.

"Cyze, maybe this dog needs food." Harper's ears perked up at the word food. He didn't know what these creatures would feed him, but he was quite hungry. He'd be quiet for a little while if they fed him something good.

"Hmmm," Cyze thought out loud. "Do we have anything that a dog could eat?" Cyze asked walking around the house looking in every corner. "I know that they can't eat certain foods."

"I'll check in the refrigerator. I'm sure that the human

who lived here has some food." Zork said and exited the room. Harper looked through the bars of his cage and out of a window and noticed that it was quite dark outside. Were Joseph and Jessica still out there searching for him? Harper cared for Joseph deeply and he knew that Joseph was probably sad that he was not there.

Harper laid down flat on his stomach and whimpered. If he ever saw Joseph again, he wouldn't bite at his pants legs or wouldn't bark at Jessica. He wouldn't run off on his own and he would be nicer to Jessica.

"There was a piece of bologna in the refrigerator, I'm guessing that the human either doesn't shop much or hasn't gotten around to doing it yet." Cyze looked at the packet of bologna.

"It is high in fat and not really good for animals, but it won't hurt him. I guess if we're going to have an army of animals, we should really pick up some food for them." Zork nodded its head in agreement and slid the bologna through the bars. Joseph never allowed him to eat the weird meat, so Harper woofed it down happily. His happiness didn't last long and he immediately felt sad again.

"How much can I feed him?" Zork asked. Zork was incredibly smart, the smartest of the two. However, when it came to animals, Cyze had him beat.

"He could probably eat two more slices and be alright, but I don't know that for sure. I'll change into the human tomorrow and buy some groceries. He had some money lying around the house." Cyze said motioning for Zork to finish feeding Harper. Harper ate the last two slices happily, but he was still hungry. This wasn't enough food for him.

"I'll get the dogs water; they haven't drunk anything in a while." Zork said and disappeared again. Harper raised his paw and placed it on the bars and gave it a gentle push. There was no way that he'd be able to open it. If dogs could sigh, Harper would have sighed at that moment.

This was the worst thing that had ever happened to him. Harper thought that the creature would open up the cage and place the water bowl in it, but he was sad when the creature placed it outside of his cage, but close enough for him to drink through the bars.

"Good thinking," Cyze said. "That one might have tried to make a run for it." Harper walked over to the water and flopped down hard on his stomach. He licked the water through the bars. He was happy to have something to drink, but unhappy because this was the way that he had to drink it. Once he had enough, Harper turned on his side and went to sleep.

CHAPTER FIVE

When Harper woke up the next morning, he was hoping to find Joseph and Jessica standing in front of him and hoping that yesterday was nothing but a nightmare, but unfortunately he was still living in his nightmare.

He woke up and was feeling a bit stiff all over. His cage was too small and he was really beginning to feel cramped. He looked at the other cages and they all were much larger than his. He might have been small, but he needed his space too.

Harper looked around for any sign of the creatures being around and was surprised when he saw none. Did these things sleep like humans? Harper didn't know for sure, but if they did he'd try to break free while they were asleep.

Harped scooted back as far as possible and then ran forward ramming his head against the bars. Harper fell in the cage, feeling quite dizzy. When he stopped seeing stars, his small mouth wrapped around the bars and tugged, but nothing happened.

Harper found a way out of everything and he was irritated that he couldn't figure out how to break free from the cage. His teeth hurt when he tried to bite it and his head throbbed when he head-butted it. All of his usual plans did not work! There was still some water left in his bowl, so he placed his small face against the bars and extended his tongue out to drink the water.

"Well, you're the first to awaken." Harper looked up when he heard the voice of Cyze. "You're a rather clever dog, so why do you resist us so much when we're trying to give you the world?"

Harper didn't want the world; he just wanted to be with his family. Harper barked. "You're going to help us inhabit this world and make it our home. You won't be thinking about those humans once we've given you everything you want."

Harper didn't know what the creature was saying, but he knew it had to be bad. "You'll grow used to us soon and then we'll become your new masters." Harper's bark grew louder. He did understand the word master and he needed to let the creature know that he'd never see them as his masters.

Cyze grinned, almost like he understood what the dog was thinking. "You'll forget them soon enough and that's a promise." Cyze walked away from his cage and went over to the blue square screen. He typed something into it and then turned around at the sound of Zork's voice.

"You got to get them food today. These dogs haven't eaten in two days." Zork said pointing towards the dogs on the opposite side of Harper.

"Yeah, yeah," Cyze said and pulled out some odd device with a big red button. When Cyze pushed the button, Harper couldn't believe his eyes. The creature went from being this horrifying thing to being a human!

"Humans are odd looking," Zork said while shaking his head. Humans were odd? These creatures were odd looking, not humans.

"I'll be back soon," Cyze said and walked out of the room. Zork turned then to face Harper with a mischievous grin on his face.

"I bet you're surprised that Cyze was able to do that." Harper was very surprised, but he was also horrified as well. "This is a gift that we aliens have." Harper cocked his head to the side, aliens? Were these horrible creatures aliens? Harper had seen people on television who acted like they were aliens from a different planet, but he always assumed that humans made things like that up to amuse themselves.

"We have different devices and we know how to change things in order to make these things more useful," Zork crouched down on the floor in front of Harper's cage. "And that is what we're going to do to you and the other animals."

Harper couldn't let the aliens change him. He enjoyed being a dog and he didn't want to become a human like Cyze. Harper began barking loudly. He wanted someone to hear him. He needed someone to hear him.

"I know what you're trying to do," Zork said moving away from the cage and placing his hands over his ears. "We've sound proofed the house while you were sleeping." Harper couldn't hear what Zork had just said because he continued to bark loudly. He barked long and hard, but there was no indication that someone had even heard him. Feeling exhausted and out of breath, Harper collapsed on the floor feeling defeated.

"I'm back," Cyze said still disguised as a human. Harper didn't even bother to look up at him.

"Good," Zork said nodding to his brother. "Don't give this one any food, I think his name was Harper." Cyze looked over at Harper, but Harper remained in his spot with his eyes on the floor.

"He gave you a problem?"

"Yes, and now he will be punished." Being with the aliens was punishment enough. Harper was beginning to accept that he and the other dogs wouldn't be saved. Several other dogs had awakened and apparently had gone back to normal because they began barking angrily. Harper wasn't even in the mood to join in with the unhappy dogs. Instead, Harper decided to go back to sleep.

###

When Harper opened his eyes again, he noticed that the other dogs were out of their cage. Harper jumped up at this. Were the aliens letting them go? Harper's tongue hung out of his mouth and he began wagging his tail. He hoped that the aliens were letting them go. As Harper watched the dogs intently, he noticed something odd about them. It wasn't anything wrong with the dogs themselves, but they were wearing something metal.

"Stand on your hind legs," Human Cyze said and the dogs listened and stood on their hind legs. "Bark!" the dogs barked in unison. Harper didn't know what had happened, but it didn't look good.

"Very good," Zork said coming out of the shadows. "Well little Harper…" Zork said when he noticed Harper watching the other dogs in confusion. "You're just a little sleepy head." Zork shook his head and smiled.

"The modification doesn't react correctly if it's attached onto an animal while they're sleeping." That wasn't a word that Harper was used to hearing. What exactly is a modification? Is it that metal suit the other dogs were wearing?

"Trust me; you were the first dog I thought of to test the modification out on." Harper barked. Zork's grinned widened.

"Should we put it on him now, brother?" Zork shook his head.

"No, let's give him a little more time since he just woke up." Harper backed away from the front of the cage and lied down with his eyes closed. He didn't want to see the dogs because they didn't look like normal dogs. Harper feared turning into whatever it was the other dogs were turning into.

"I can't wait to have this dog under our control, I want to take away all of his hope, his dreams." Cyze said as he walked around in a circle with the other animals following behind him.

"Soon brother, soon."

CHAPTER SIX

Harper watched the other animals follow the aliens' instructions for what seemed like hours. He was getting tired of looking at them and he was feeling rather hungry. The aliens hadn't fed him at all that day because they were punishing him. He wasn't used to going long periods without being fed. Joseph and Jessica always made sure that he had water and food. He wondered how long it had been since he had seen them.

Harper began to pace around the small cage. He wanted to keep his mind off of his hunger and off of his present predicament. Harper hadn't made a single sound in hours. He was broken; the aliens had broken his pride and taken away all of his happiness.

"Go ahead and feed him now," Zork said to Cyze. "He's been acting okay." Cyze walked into the other room, taking Harper's bowl with him. "Did you feed the cat?" Harper's ears shot up. The aliens had captured a cat as well?!

"Yes, Killer's eaten a little while ago. She's such a good animal, so much different than these dogs." Cyze said placing the bowl in front of Harper's cage. Harper licked at the food through the bars.

"It's a shame the modifications doesn't work on Killer. She'd be great at helping us inhabit the world."

"I'm sure there's a way for us to modify her, we just haven't figured it out yet." Harper was concerned about what the aliens were saying, but he was hungry which made him lose his interest in them. It was harder for him to eat his food through the bars, but he managed to eat every bite. After he was done he had some of his water as well. The aliens' might have been mean to him when it came to feeding him, but they continued to give him fresh water.

"Let's try now while he's relaxed," Harper saw his cage doors opening and before he was able to take off running, Cyze had grabbed him. Harper began barking loudly.

"Hurry up and modify the dog!" Zork yelled. "His barks are giving me a headache." Cyze grabbed Harper around the mouth and squeezed it shut. Harper's barks turned into whimpers.

"Pass me a muzzle"

"That's what we've should've done in the first place." Zork said and handed Cyze the muzzle. Releasing his hand around Harper's mouth, before he started to bark again, the muzzle was secured around his face. "Finally," Zork said and stood up. "Can you handle things here? I want to go over to the other location that we've secured.

"Yes, this house may be a little too small, but it is always good to have options." Zork nodded his head and pulled a device out of his pocket.

"When the modifications are in place and works better, bring the animals to me."

"Yes, I will bring them over to that majestic blue house when I am done with the experiments." Zork smiled at Cyze, pushed the button, and was gone. Harper tried to bark again, but the muzzle held his mouth in place. "Now let's deal with you, little one."

Harper shivered in fear. He looked at the other dogs then and noticed that their eyes were dark red. The dogs were no longer dogs, but something much more. Harper didn't want anything to do with the aliens' experiments.

"Here we are," Cyze said grabbing a cylinder object from off of the table. Harper could make out the letters M.O.D. but Cyze was covering the other letters with his hand. Cyze aimed it Harper and Harper whimpered and squirmed.

"You're not getting away," as soon as Cyze said that, the object wrapped itself tightly around Harper's body.

Placing the small dog on a nearby table, Harper wasn't able to move or even stand up.

"Ha! It's working!" Cyze yelled with joy apparent on his face. Harper was anything but joyful as the object tightened its hold on him. After a while, Harper began seeing red and his pain started to slowly drift away. He was able to stand a little after a few minutes and his breathing returned to normal.

Harper started to feel at ease and he began feeling comfortable. Cyze backed up away from Harper and Harper's eyes followed him lazily. Cyze picked up a remote and pushed a button.

"Come to me," he demanded and Harper felt his legs move in the direction of Cyze's voice. It was almost like his body had a mind of its own. "Stand in the line with your brothers!" Harper obeyed and joined the other animals in line. Harper's head felt fuzzy and he was having a hard time remembering things. "Bark," he called out and the animals barked.

"Stand on your hind legs," Harper stood on his hind legs and he felt as if they had gotten stronger. Or were his legs always like this? He just could not remember. "Run around the room," even though Harper was the smallest dog in the house, Harper ran around the room twice before the other dogs had made it around once. "Very good, come back to me."

Harper began to feel like this was normal and that he did

this every day. This alien's face filled every inch of his memories and he completely forgotten about Joseph, the most important human in the world to him. "I want you all to listen," Cyze said seriously. "We will train until you are perfect! This world would be ours as long as each of you does your part." The dogs barked their agreement.

"Whatever I say you shall do without hesitation." The dogs barked again. "When I say flee, you'll flee. When I say jump, you'll jump. When I sat attack, you will attack!" Cyze said this louder so the dogs barked louder. "I am your master and you will obey me!" The dogs howled as their leader spoke. Some part of Harper's consciousness was still there, screaming at him to come back to his senses. He couldn't hear the voice though; the animal's howls were too loud.

"Now I want you all to return to your cages until I come back," Harper and the rest of the animals began walking back to the cages that they came into the house in. The doors shut quickly and a clicking noise could be heard throughout the room. "I've found another brother for you, a Jack Russell," Cyze looked over at Harper. "This dog would be a great friend to you."

With that said, Cyze disappeared. All was silent. Even Harper did as he was told and he still couldn't hear the voice in his head screaming that they needed to get out of there and find Joseph and Jessica. Harper was losing his true self and the metal wrapped around his body was draining his true self quicker with each passing second.

Even though Harper couldn't hear his true self any longer, somewhere deep down inside of him craved to be free. He wanted to be free to see Joseph again, swim in the water by the cabin, and even be held by Jessica again. His red eyes focused on nothing and the normally loud part of his brain was silent. It had gotten dark when Cyze brought home the new dog in a bag. The animals red eyes welcomed the newcomer.

Hearing the little dog's frightened whimpers brought a little of Harper's sanity back, but he lost it just as quick. Harper's last bit of consciousness cried out that he wanted to be free. What Harper didn't know was that the dog outside of the house looking in, would set him and the rest of the dogs free soon.

CHARLIE
BOOK

Made in the USA
San Bernardino, CA
17 May 2018